THIS WALKER BOOK BELONGS TO:

_____

_____

_____

_____

For Jenny Hawkesworth M.C.

For Elizabeth C.G.

First published 1980
by Walker Books Ltd
87 Vauxhall Walk
London SE11 5HJ

This edition published 1998

2 4 6 8 10 9 7 5 3

Text © 1980 Mirabel Cecil
Illustrations © 1980 Christina Gascoigne

This book has been typeset in Baskerville.

Printed in Hong Kong/China

British Library Cataloguing in Publication Data
A catalogue record for this book is
available from the British Library.

ISBN 0-7445-6385-2

RUBY
the
Christmas Donkey

Mirabel Cecil

ILLUSTRATED BY Christina Gascoigne

WALKER BOOKS
AND SUBSIDIARIES
LONDON · BOSTON · SYDNEY

Ruby and Scarlett were two donkeys who spent their summers giving rides to children on the beach.

They had been doing this for many years, especially Ruby, who was the older of the two donkeys.

But one summer, Ruby was not chosen for rides nearly as often as Scarlett. Ruby was not as strong as she had been, and could only plod slowly along the sands. So Scarlett carried the children, while Ruby waited for her to come back.

Much of the time, Ruby stood alone.

Both the donkeys looked forward to the end of summer. They knew they would spend a peaceful autumn in a field.

Old Ruby was particularly pleased at the good rest.

Sometimes the children who lived nearby came to see Ruby and Scarlett. They brought the donkeys crusts and carrots to eat.

Ruby moved more and more slowly.

Winter came. The little creatures who
lived nearby grew warm coats or got
ready to sleep through the cold months.

Ruby was too old to grow a warm coat.
"Why not run round as I do?" said
Scarlett. But Ruby could not.

Tears trickled down Ruby's soft, grey nose. They turned to icicles before they reached the ground.

Ruby bowed her shaggy, old head in the bitter wind. She thought of the hot summers she had spent on the beach, and wondered whether she would ever enjoy the sunshine again.

"I never thought I would end my days in this cold misery," she complained to Scarlett.

The little animals were usually fast asleep now, but they could not rest while their old friend Ruby was so unhappy. They decided that since she could not make a warm winter coat for herself, they would make one for her!

Mice collected pine cones, birds got pine
needles and hares made piles of wool.

The mole woke up. The dormice, shrew
and birds put everything into heaps.

Rabbits hopped quickly to the hares
with wool from the sheep while
hedgehogs and rats gathered leaves.

Squirrels brought acorns and grasses,
and the weasel gave directions.

Soon it was time to make the coat.
Hedgehogs, mice, rats and squirrels
wove the grasses on to a branch.

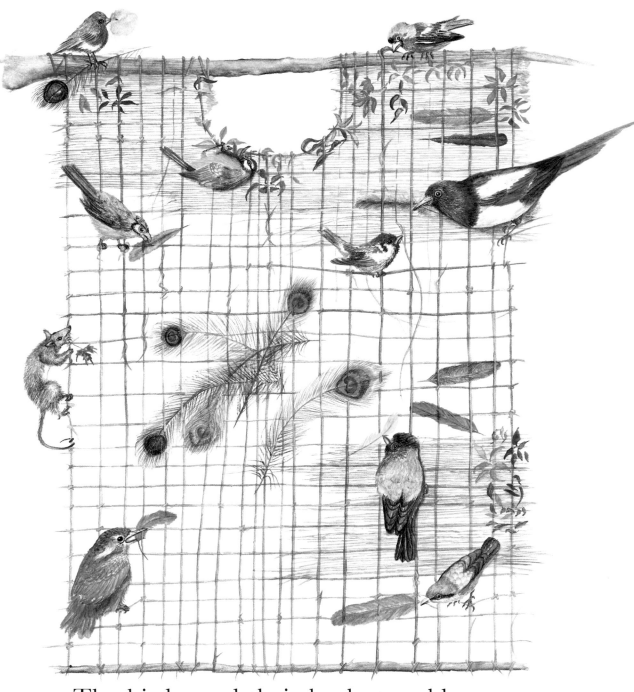

The birds used their beaks to add
the feathers, wool and leaves.
At last the coat was finished!

The weasel blew his whistle to
wake the owl, who was big enough
and strong enough to lift up the coat.
· The owl picked up the coat with
the help of the other birds.
    Silently, they flew off.

Ruby lay on the frosty ground,
trying to keep warm. She did not
hear the swish of the birds' wings,
or see the weasel directing the owl.
Ruby did not even notice all the
animals gathered round her.

When the birds dropped the coat on to
her, Ruby thought it was a present that
had fallen out of the snowy sky.

It was a wonderful coat, a magic coat!
"Now I'll never be cold again," Ruby
said, as she thanked all the animals.

The next day the children came down to the field with carrots and crusts for the donkeys. They were going to choose one donkey to be in a Nativity play they were giving that night.

Would it be Scarlett? Or Ruby?

Last year Scarlett had been chosen, and so now she came forward eagerly to the gate. But one of the boys noticed Ruby's coat at once.

"Look!" he shouted to the others. "Look at Ruby's magic coat! We must have her in the Nativity play!"

So the children led Ruby out of the
field towards the school where everyone
was busy getting ready for the play.

Scarlett and the other animals watched
as Ruby left. They were very proud of
the coat they had made her.

That night, as the snow fell softly, all the animals went up to the school. They gathered round the lighted window to watch the play. Even the mole managed to stay awake. And the weasel made sure that everyone was quiet.

They saw all the children dressed in their costumes. But Ruby did not have to dress up. She was perfect as she was, in her magic coat, with the peacock feathers that glowed like jewels.

Best of all, Ruby would never be cold again. She had her coat of wool and feathers, and grasses and leaves.

MORE WALKER PAPERBACKS
For You to Enjoy

A CHRISTMAS CAROL
by Charles Dickens

Abridged by Vivian French, illustrated by Patrick Benson

A skilfully abridged, stunningly illustrated version for children
of one of the most popular of all Christmas stories.

"A most handsome edition … with wonderful ghosts." *Books for Keeps*

0-7445-6021-7   £4.99

CAN IT BE TRUE?
by Susan Hill, illustrated by Angela Barrett

Winner of the Smarties Book Prize (6 – 8 years)

"Evokes, in a prose poem of marvellous concision, the real spirit
of Christmas Eve … beautiful illustrations."
The Sunday Telegraph

0-7445-1721-4   £4.99

THE GOOD LITTLE CHRISTMAS TREE
by Ursula Moray Williams, illustrated by Gillian Tyler

First published in 1943, this classic tale about a heroic little Christmas
tree has been newly illustrated, making it more enchanting than ever.

"The perfect Christmas book. This timeless tale captures
the spirit of the season." *The Lady*

0-7445-2355-9   £4.99